Mel Bay's

# Anyone Can Improv[illegible]

by Matt Dennis

An Original Study for Piano of
THE POP AND JAZZ STANDARD

Includes the Internationally Known
Pop/Jazz Standard
"ANGEL EYES"

DEDICATION...
I dedicate this study to a fine musician,
gentleman and my good friend MEL BAY.
Matt Dennis



Visit us on the Web at www.melbay.com — E-mail us at email@melbay.com

# Contents

# *Notes by Matt Dennis*

## WHAT IS A POPULAR STANDARD?

The most performed and lasting Popular Songs of the past years, the Ballads, Folk Songs, Rhythm and Broadway Musical Songs, also many in the Public Domain, have become what are called POP (Popular) STANDARDS. These are the songs loved by the public, which have caught on and seem to live forever, due to some magical spark from the minds of the original composers and lyricists, stirring up nostalgic memories, making such songs unforgettable.

An occasional instrumental piece, without lyrics, makes its way into the POP STANDARD category, such as an orchestral, solo, or Big Band instrumental... a theme from a motion picture or a well known strain from a classical selection, etc. A lyric, sometimes, is added making the song or piece even more popular.

Certain of these songs have a special quality apart from the usual, attracting the ears and imagination of Singers, Musicians and Arrangers who think along IMPROVISATIONAL lines. It may be an unusual melody, more interesting musical chords, etc. If the piece has a lyric it could be meaningful and worth remembering, as a reminder of the original emotion and phrasing of the selection, a help when improvising.

## WHAT IS A JAZZ STANDARD?

Many POP STANDARDS become JAZZ STANDARDS due to the construction of the song, and tempo or beat. Such songs are picked up by Blues and Jazz Pianists, Singers, Instrumental Soloists and Arrangers, all sensing something different about the song or piece and giving it their own identifiable sound, when IMPROVISING. Such renditions remain popular thru the years, on recordings, from "live" performances in concerts, clubs and Radio or TV, establishing the song or piece as a JAZZ STANDARD, and worth perpetuating. The JAZZ STANDARD is a natural on which to IMPROVISE, being so familiar to such artists. With this influence, each succeeding generation of Pop and Jazz Artists will tend to perform such music in their own individual styles. Fortunately, new music continues to be introduced, always adding to the wonderful heritage of the POP and JAZZ STANDARD. The JAZZ STANDARD usually has a more definite beat than the POP STANDARD, and at times a more complex set of chords, offering the artist more IMPROVISATIONAL possibilities.

The average traditional POP or JAZZ STANDARD has 32 Bars (measures); some Blues have 12 or 16 Bars, and thanks to the genius of the likes of COLE PORTER, JEROME KERN and other inspired Broadway Show writers, we have great POP and JAZZ STANDARDS running anywhere from 12 to 72 Bars. This affords a real challenge to the Jazz Pianist or instrumentalist when improvising to the original song form. There are many memorable recordings of how this is done.

## GIANTS OF JAZZ PIANO

Legendary artists who have most influenced the Jazz Pianist have been the likes of ART TATUM, "FATS" WALLER, DUKE ELLINGTON and EARL HINES... not forgetting some of today's fine pianists, OSCAR PETERSON, HANK JONES, GEORGE SHEARING, PAUL SMITH, ANDRE PREVIN and BILLY TAYLOR . Did you know that the famed Composer GEORGE GERSHWIN (writer of many world famous STANDARDS) played some pretty darned good Jazz Piano? He had a great mind for improvisation, and original melody and chord conception... very inventive! Hearing the music of these artists is a rich experience, a wonderful influence, and you can learn techniques... sounds, and profit by understanding *their* choice of JAZZ and POP STANDARDS, and *their* interpretations.

## FAVORITE JAZZ STANDARDS

While there are countless JAZZ STANDARDS on recall to the mind of the Professional Jazz Pianist, too numerous to list here, a group of select songs comes to my own mind, based on my own personal experiences of playing piano (and singing) with leading Jazz Pros. Keep in mind that many POP STANDARDS become JAZZ STANDARDS. I have fun with these songs when I sit down to improvise at the piano, knowing and feeling instinctively each song's construction and intention. Therefore, I am at complete liberty to experiment and freshly improvise over the original chords, to create new melodic, harmonic and rhythmic ideas.

By using Altered, Added and Substitution Chords, and "sympathetic" Chord Voicings it is almost like composing a new song or piece, and so I can play several choruses, one after the other, with no two choruses sounding alike. When a lyric is available I try to keep it in mind, as this puts me in tune with the poetic feeling so that when I take musical liberties with the piece, in a treatment, I will respect the intent of the Lyricist as well as the Composer. There is a definite influence here.

Monumental JAZZ STANDARDS... favorites, and on instant recall by the PRO JAZZ PIANIST; a necessary bit of repertoire. Originally Popular Songs, they have become POP & JAZZ STANDARDS:

BLUE SKIES
*By Irving Berlin*

LADY BE GOOD
I'VE GOT RHYTHM
EMBRACEABLE YOU
A FOGGY DAY
*Music: George Gershwin*
*Lyric: Ira Gershwin*

YESTERDAYS
ALL THE THINGS YOU ARE
*Music: Jerome Kern*
*Lyric: Oscar Hammerstein II*

TEA FOR TWO
*Music: Vincent Youmans*
*Lyric: Irving Caesar*

I GET A KICK OUT OF YOU
IT'S ALL RIGHT WITH ME
JUST ONE OF THOSE THINGS
NIGHT AND DAY
*By Cole Porter*

AUTUMN IN NEW YORK
*Music: Vernon Duke*

I CAN'T GET STARTED WITH YOU
*Music: Vernon Duke*
*Lyric: Ira Gershwin*

BODY AND SOUL
*Music: John Green*
*Lyric: Edward Heyman*

HERE'S THAT RAINY DAY
POLKA DOTS AND MOONBEAMS
IMAGINATION
*Music: James Van Heusen*
*Lyric: Johnny Burke*

HONEYSUCKLE ROSE
*Music: "Fats" Waller*
*Lyric: Andy Razaf*

SATIN DOLL
*By Duke Ellington*

BLUE MOON
DANCING ON THE CEILING
I COULD WRITE A BOOK
MOUNTAIN GREENERY
*Music: Richard Rodgers*
*Lyric: Lorenz Hart*

Great songs by famous ASCAP writers, and just touching the surface. I am a member of this fine organization, myself, and have had the good fortune that several of my own original songs fell into such a POP & JAZZ STANDARD bag, over the years... an entirely unpredictable happening and a tremendous compliment to a songwriter. These songs I composed, with outstanding lyrics by my still active co-writer Tom Adair, are: EVERYTHING HAPPENS TO ME, LET'S GET AWAY FROM IT ALL, WILL YOU STILL BE MINE? VIOLETS FOR YOUR FURS and THE NIGHT WE CALLED IT A DAY. Then, there's my song ANGEL EYES, with the potent lyric by Earl Brent.

Composed as Popular Songs, they became POP & JAZZ STANDARDS. Nice to know that your songs are requested and performed by talented POP & JAZZ artists the world over.

## BUILD YOUR JAZZ REPERTOIRE

It is important that you build a repertoire of the most known and requested JAZZ & POP STANDARDS, to play piano like the PROS. This means you should MEMORIZE each song so that it becomes second nature to play it... learn the construction of the melody, harmony (chords) and structure (form) of the song. Listen to the songs whenever possible on recordings, or in "live" performances by the best Jazz Pianists. This will develop your musical taste and expertise to your benefit when playing your own improvisational Jazz Piano.

## ORIGINAL EXAMPLES OF THE JAZZ STANDARD

In the following pages of this folio are original songs, some with lyrics, arranged in the style of some of the best known JAZZ STANDARDS, and planned in FOUR STEPS to give you the experience of COMPING and IMPROVISING. FOUR arrangements of EACH SONG, OR PIECE.

FOUR STEPS:

**STEP #1 THE SHEET MUSIC**

The traditional Sheet Music arrangement of a song, for Voice and Piano, with lyric (words) and music, written on 3 stave lines. Top stave for Voice, bottom 2 staves for Piano. Note that the Piano part is complete within itself... the melody is always present, so that the player has the choice of playing solo piano or along with a singer or instrumentalist using the Voice stave. The chords are stated above the melody or Voice line. Eventually, as we progress with the various steps we shall drop the *Sheet Music* version and work directly from the *Lead Sheet* (see later explanation).

**STEP #2 COMPING**

Playing piano accompaniment to a soloist, or as in a combo or band. By following the same chord line as shown in the Sheet Music arrangement (also in the Lead Sheet... explained later), we now avoid the actual melody, and will rearrange and revoice the chords in such a manner that we are accompanying the original melody without actually playing the melody ourself.

We must be familiar with chord voicing and inversions to play in this fashion, allowing the soloist the freedom to phrase the melody and interpret the piece with their own feeling and in their own style.

Here, we are playing supportive chords in a rhythmic pattern, with an occasional "fill" where there might be an opening at the end of a melodic phrase. We have cued-in the Melody from the Sheet Music arrangement as a convenient guide so you can *see* how you are COMPING or following the actual melody or solo line above.

**STEP #3 JAZZ IMPROV**

This is an improvised version of the song, showing what you can do with ALTERED, ADDED and SUBSTITUTION CHORDS, as we come up with a newly invented melody line, revoicing the original chords to fit, and punctuating the rhythm with accented chordal offbeats, still keeping in *mind* the original song, tempo or beat. Note that you are improvising *relative* to the original, but flattering or expanding the form and chords. It is necessary that you know your material so well you will have complete freedom for your ideas. The original melody and structure of the song or piece should always be in the back of your mind while you are creating your own treatment. The FUN part is that once you learn how to do this you are *exploring* with unlimited possibilities.

You are, in effect, making up counter-melodies to the original. You should always enjoy sitting down to your own piano improvisations, never knowing what might come up next.

We might use BLOCK chords, played rhythmicly, and sometimes the left hand will play an accent chord to support your Jazz melodic line. Think also in *phrases* so your IMPROV will have continuity. Your new chords should be extensions of the original chords... it all depends on how deeply you are into your understanding of the fine chordal possibilities as used in Jazz and Contemporary music.

The best Jazz Pianists are appreciated for their inventive ideas and for what they can do with a known song or piece. Get up on their sounds... it took them years to establish their styles and you can profit by their experience.

**STEP #4 THE LEAD SHEET**

A condensed version of the Sheet Music, just the melody with chords named above, with lyric (unless the piece is an instrumental)... one stave... no piano part. This is what the PROS use, generally, when playing over a song, and is sufficient enough to work with when COMPING or IMPROVISING. The PROS, being familiar with chords by name, can fill out the piano, using their own chord voicings, inversions, and playing the piece in a complete full style. This is the ultimate in IMPROVISATION on a given melody, with chords stated.

The popular FAKE books, containing the "leads" of the best known POP and JAZZ STANDARDS, contain many songs due to the condensed LEAD SHEET versions. Professional musicians, singers and arrangers are used to this form and the more familiar YOU are with the chords the easier you will be able to play in this fashion, from the LEAD SHEET... and the more inventive will be your IMPROV. You are *REALLY ON YOUR OWN* when you arrive at *THE LEAD SHEET.*

# "Lulu Belle"

Sheet Music

Words by Tom Adair
A.S.C.A.P.

Music by Matt Dennis
A.S.C.A.P.

Fmaj9 D7-9 Gm7 C7sus4 add9 B♭○ Am7 D+7-9
Lu - lu Belle, she's got a style has Lu - lu Belle,
Gm7 C+7-9 A+7 D9 (G+7)
and I fell for the lilt of her voice, had no choice
G+7 C9 -9 (F6) F6 B♭9add6 (Fmaj9)
but go tag - gin' a - long.
Fmaj9 nc B Bass G7/B B♭m6 Am7 D+7-9
I just don't know the words to des - cribe her,
3

G7/B
Bbm6
Am7
Gm7 Fmaj7
Gm7 Am7 (Bbm7)
She's got a charm all her own.
Bbm7
Eb7-9
(Abmaj7)
Abmaj7
Db9
She's so high line, needs no by line, where -
no C
Cmaj9/E
G+7
(C7sus4 add9)
C7sus4 add9
C7-9
ev - er we go she's known.
Fmaj9
D7-9
Gm7
C7sus4 add9
Bb°
Lu - lu Belle, no - bo - dy knows and

Am7 D+7-9 Gm7 C7-9 (A+7)
I won't tell that she's mine, and I'll al -
A+7 D9 (G9 + 5) G9+5 C9 C7-9 (F6)
- ways be true to my own lovely Lu - lu Belle.
1. F6 D+7-9 G9add6 C+7-9
2. F6 B♭m11 Fmaj9

# "Lulu Belle"

Comping

Words: Tom Adair
A.S.C.A.P.

Music: Matt Dennis
A.S.C.A.P.

Fmaj9
D7-9
Gm7
C7(9)sus4
B♭○
Am7
D+7-9
Gm7
C+7-9
A7+5
D9
G9+5
C9
-9
3
(Soloist "pick-ups")
F6
B♭9
F6
B Bass
G7/B
B♭m6
Am7
D Bass
D+7-9

B Bass G7/B
B♭m6
Am7
A♭m7 Gm7 Fmaj7
Gm7 Am7 B♭m7
E♭7-9
A♭maj7
D♭9
no C
Cmaj9
G+7
C7(9)sus4
C7-9
Fmaj9
D7-9
Gm7
C7sus4 add9
B♭o
Am7
D+7-9

Notice, especially, the voicing of the chords, in accompaniment to the "cued-in melody." You will find that both hands are playing an independent musical line of thought in support of and flattering the solo lead or melody. Continuity, and of course originality, will be both important in the background phrases you will play. The greater part of the chord voicing will be with the right hand in the treble clef, due to playing in the middle register of the piano, while the left hand has it's own bass line and yet plays fundamental notes to give the harmony it's bottom, basic sound. Less notes are always played, but structually important "frame of the chord" notes, with the left hand___ due to the lower register on the piano, for clarity of the harmony. Where a lead note is held (melody) the pianist has the opportunity to "fill" for the proper beats . . . respecting, of course, the necessary chord changes.

# "Lulu Belle"

**Jazz Improv**

**Words - Tom Adair**
**A.S.C.A.P.**

**Music - Matt Dennis**
**A.S.C.A.P.**

Gm7
no C
C9/E
-9
G
A
Bass
A+7
no D
D9/F♯
♭9
G7add6
G7
C9
no C
C7+5(9)
no F
Fmaj9
A
nc
4
B♭m11
no F
Fmaj7/C
nc
3
5
no G
Gmaj9/B
B♭m6
nc
Am7
D7♭5-9
nc
B○
B♭○
nc
A♭m7
Gm7
Fmaj7
nc
B♭m7
nc
E♭7-9
nc
Cm7
nc
sus4
D♭7(9)
D♭9
no C
Cmaj9
E
nc
G7
+9
+5
C Bass
C7add6
C7+9
+5
C7

**Compare:**

See how we improvise a melody line, with added chords and a moving bass line . . . all compatable and flattering to the original sheet music & lead sheet versions.

**Sheet Music**

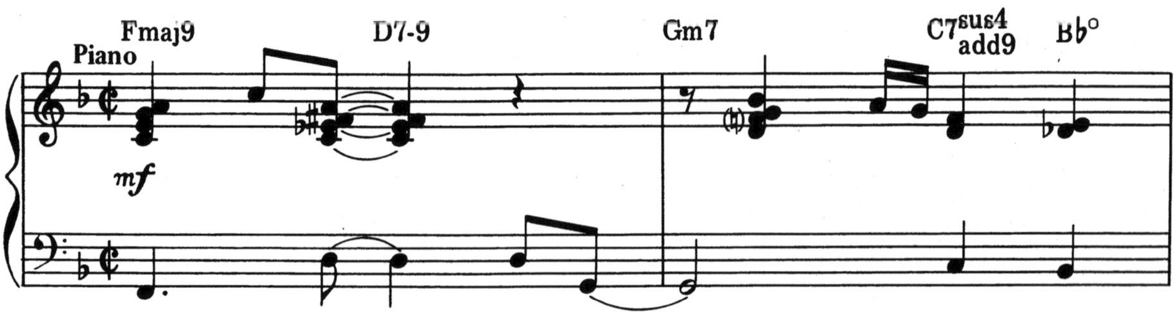


**Jazz Improv**

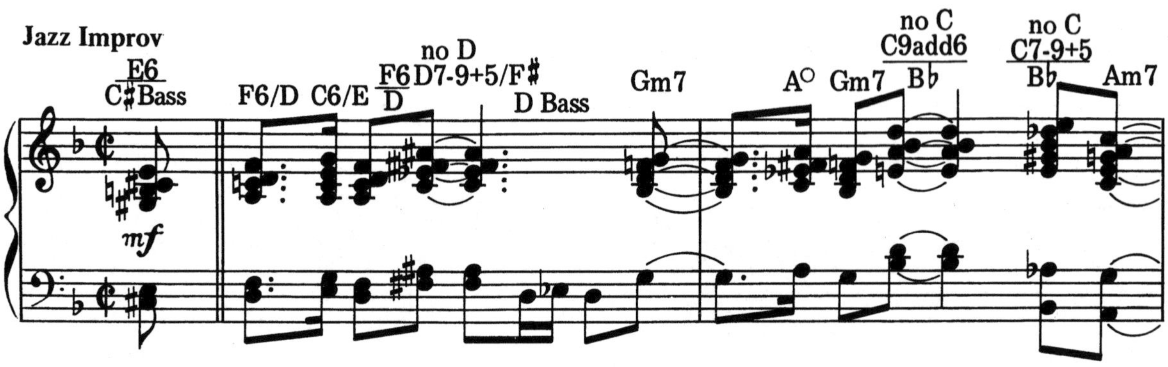

# "Lulu Belle"

Lead Sheet

Words: Tom Adair
A.S.C.A.P.

Music: Matt Dennis
A.S.C.A.P.

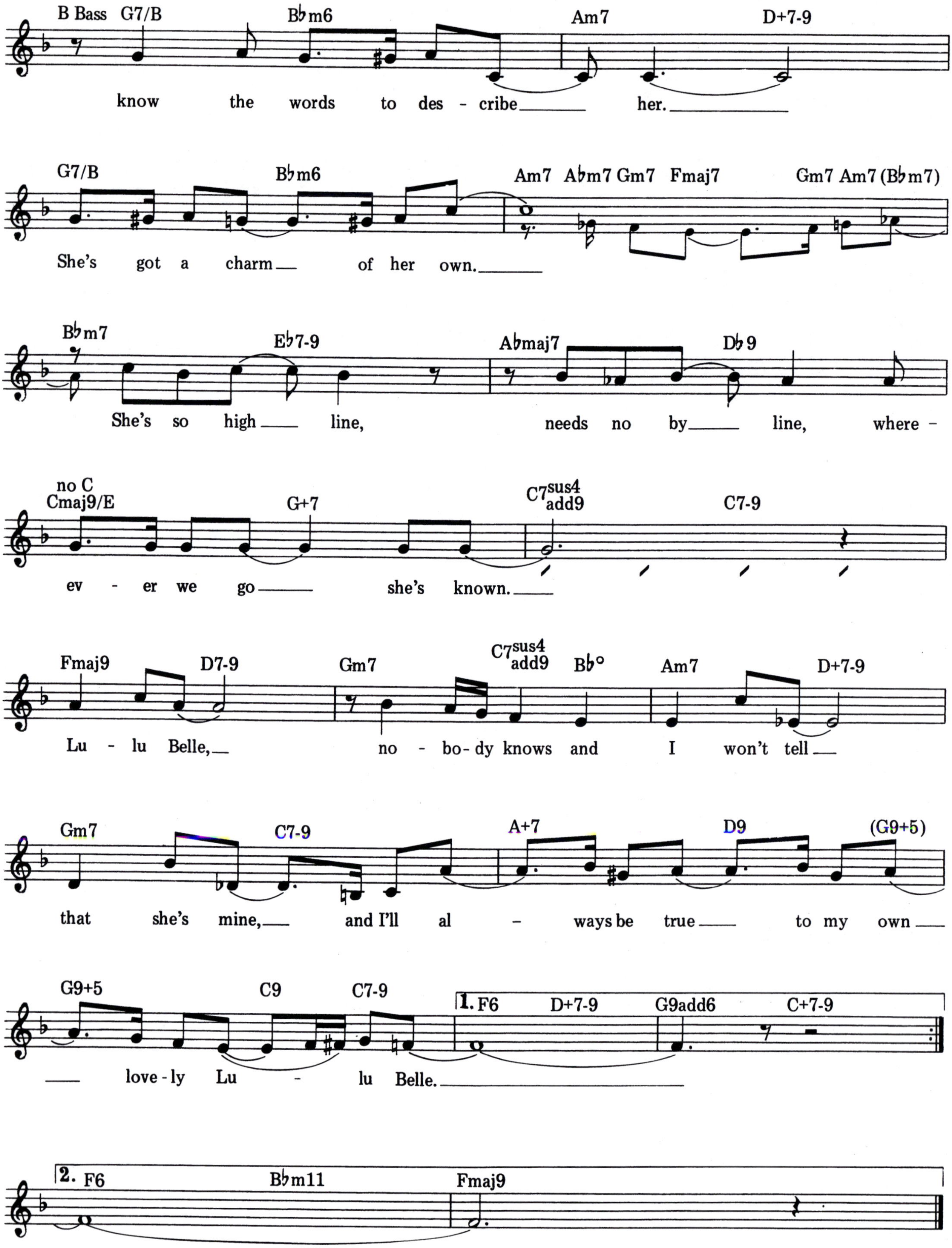
B Bass G7/B
Bbm6
Am7
D+7-9
know the words to des - cribe her.
G7/B
Bbm6
Am7 Abm7 Gm7 Fmaj7
Gm7 Am7 (Bbm7)
She's got a charm of her own.
Bbm7
Eb7-9
Abmaj7
Db9
She's so high line, needs no by line, where -
no C
Cmaj9/E
G+7
C7sus4 add9
C7-9
ev - er we go she's known.
Fmaj9
D7-9
Gm7
C7sus4 add9
Bb°
Am7
D+7-9
Lu - lu Belle, no - bo- dy knows and I won't tell
Gm7
C7-9
A+7
D9
(G9+5)
that she's mine, and I'll al - ways be true to my own
G9+5
C9
C7-9
1. F6
D+7-9
G9add6
C+7-9
love - ly Lu - lu Belle.
2. F6
Bbm11
Fmaj9

# "No Name Blues"

Sheet Music (no lyric)

(Melody is obvious, in treble clef)

by Matt Dennis
A.S.C.A.P.

Since there is no lyric to this piece, it would be classed as an instrumental solo. The sheet music shows the melody as played by the piano. When "comping" it is as if you were accompanying a solo instrument. The "improv" arrangement will show you how to play around with the original theme, as you do on the other pieces where there is a lyric . . . the stated chord progressions are your source for improvisation. The "lead sheet" puts you on your own, to invent freely as ideas come to you.

# "No Name Blues"

**Comping Arr.**

Composed and arr. by Matt Dennis
A.S.C.A.P.

(A+/C♯)
Dm7/C
G9/B♮
B♭m6 F/A
D♭7/A♭
Gm7
C7sus4 add9, 11, 13
F
F6(9) C
B♭m7
B♭m6
no F Fmaj7/C
F6
F
Fmaj7
F7
B♭m11
Am7
Gm7
G♭7
Fmaj7
G+7-9
C9
F
F
Fmaj7/E
(6) F7/E♭
B♭m7
3

Am7
Gm7
G♭7
Fmaj7
F6
nc
E Bass
Gm6/E
B♭9
A9
Dm
A+/C♯
Dm7/C
no G
G9/B♮
B♭m(6)
F/A
D♭7/A♭
Gm7
C7sus4 add9,11,13
Fmaj9
B♭7sus4 add9,11
B♭m6/F add11
no F
Fmaj9 add6/E
F Bass

# "No Name Blues"

Improv Arr.

Composed and Arranged by Matt Dennis
A.S.C.A.P.

Used by permission.

no G♭
G♭9/B♭
no F
Fmaj9/A
Dm7
no G
G7-9add6/F
no C
C7+9,-13
F6/D
G7-9add6
C+7+9
F6
no C-9
Cm7/B♭
F7-9/A
no C
Cm9/E♭
F+7/E♭
no B♭
B♭m9/D♭
B♭m6
D♭
Fmaj7/C
B♭m7
C6
Dm7
no G
G7-9/F
no C
C7/E
no F
F6/D
F Bass
F9add6/A
no F
F+7-9addG♯/A
A Bass
no B♭
B♭m9/A♭
B♭Bass
no F
Fmaj9/A
nc
B♭Bass
B♭m7
Am7
nc
A♭Bass
A♭m7
Gm7
nc
G♭Bass
G♭maj7
Fmaj7
A7-9
-5

Sounding like a completely different piece, what with the new melody line and different chord changes . . . still it's all relative to the original. This is what the mind can conceive in improvising to a known piece or song . . . you must retain, in the back of your mind, the original form . . . all the changes are meant to enrich the original, expanding the melodic and harmonic possibilities wherever possible. The great jazz pianists establish their styles and personalities musically thru such improvisation. Study these styles for your own experience and influence.

# "No Name Blues"

Lead Sheet

by Matt Dennis
A.S.C.A.P.

* Slash marks indicate beats

Sheet Music

# "As Long As There's Music"

Words by Tom Adair
A.S.C.A.P.

Music by Matt Dennis
A.S.C.A.P.

Gmaj7 Am7 A#o Bm7 Em7 A9 Em7 Co(no A A7/C#)
I'll keep go - in' strong As Long As There's Mu - sic,
no A A9/C# A9 Am7 D9(6) D7-9 ((G7sus4 (9))
mu - sic, can't get e - nough
G7sus4 (9) Dm7 G7-9 add 13
of those en - chant - ing songs.
Cmaj9 F#m11 B7-9 +5
My poor head is a - whirl,

Em7 E♭+5 Dm7 G7(6) G7+5(9)/B
Kern, and Rod - gers, and ear - ly G e r s h - win;
Cmaj9 B♭9add13 A9add13 A7+5(9) (D7sus4 (9))
Ste - phen Sond - heim, Cole Por - ter too;
D7sus4(9) D7-9 +5
Man - ci - ni, don't for - get a - bout Bach - rach.
Gmaj7 Am7 A♯○ Bm7 Em7 A9 Em7/B C○ (no A A9/C♯)
Play it on a gong, a horn, or a cel - lo,

NOTE: Here we have the 1st and 2nd endings to the chorus of this piece, typical of most sheet music arrangements where there is a lyric. Instrumental pieces usually will not have this, but will be played straight thru to a natural ending . . . there are exceptions, especially in the improv arrangements.

# "As Long As There's Music"

**Comping**

Words: Tom Adair
A.S.C.A.P.

Music: Matt Dennis
A.S.C.A.P.

Used by permission.

Gmaj9
Am7
A♯○
Bm7
Em7
A9
Em7/B
C○ no A (A9/C♯)
no A A9/C♯
A9add13
Am7
D9 (6)
D7-9 (6)
D7-9 (G7sus4 (9))
G7sus4 (9)
Dm7
G7-9 add13
Cmaj9
F♯m9
B7-9 +5

Em7
E♭+5
Dm7
G7(6)
G+7/B
Cmaj9
B♭9add13
A9add13
A7(9) +5 (D7sus4 (9))
D7sus4 (9)
D7-9 +5
Gmaj9
Am7
A♯○
Bm7
Em7
nc
A Bass

A9
Em7/B
C°
no A
A9/C♯
A Bass
A9add13
Am7
D9(6)
D7-9
(G6)
1.
G6
Bm7
B♭°
Am7
A♭9♯11
2.
G6
Am7
B♭m7
no G
Gmaj9/B
Gmaj9

# "As Long As There's Music"

Jazz Improv

Words: Tom Adair
A.S.C.A.P.

Music: Matt Dennis
A.S.C.A.P.

Am7
D7sus4 add 9, 13
D9add13/F♯
D+7-9
G7sus4(9)
Dm7
no G G9add13/F♮
no G G+7-9/F♮
no C Cmaj9/E
nc(no chord)
F♯m7
B7♭9
Em7
Em
E♭+5
Dm7
no G G9add13/F♮
G+7+9
Cmaj9
B♭7add13
add9
A7add13

*We skip the 1st and 2nd endings here, as we are improvising and finish naturally in the 31st and 32nd measures.

# "As Long As There's Music"

Lead Sheet

Words by Tom Adair
A.S.C.A.P.

Music by Matt Dennis
A.S.C.A.P.

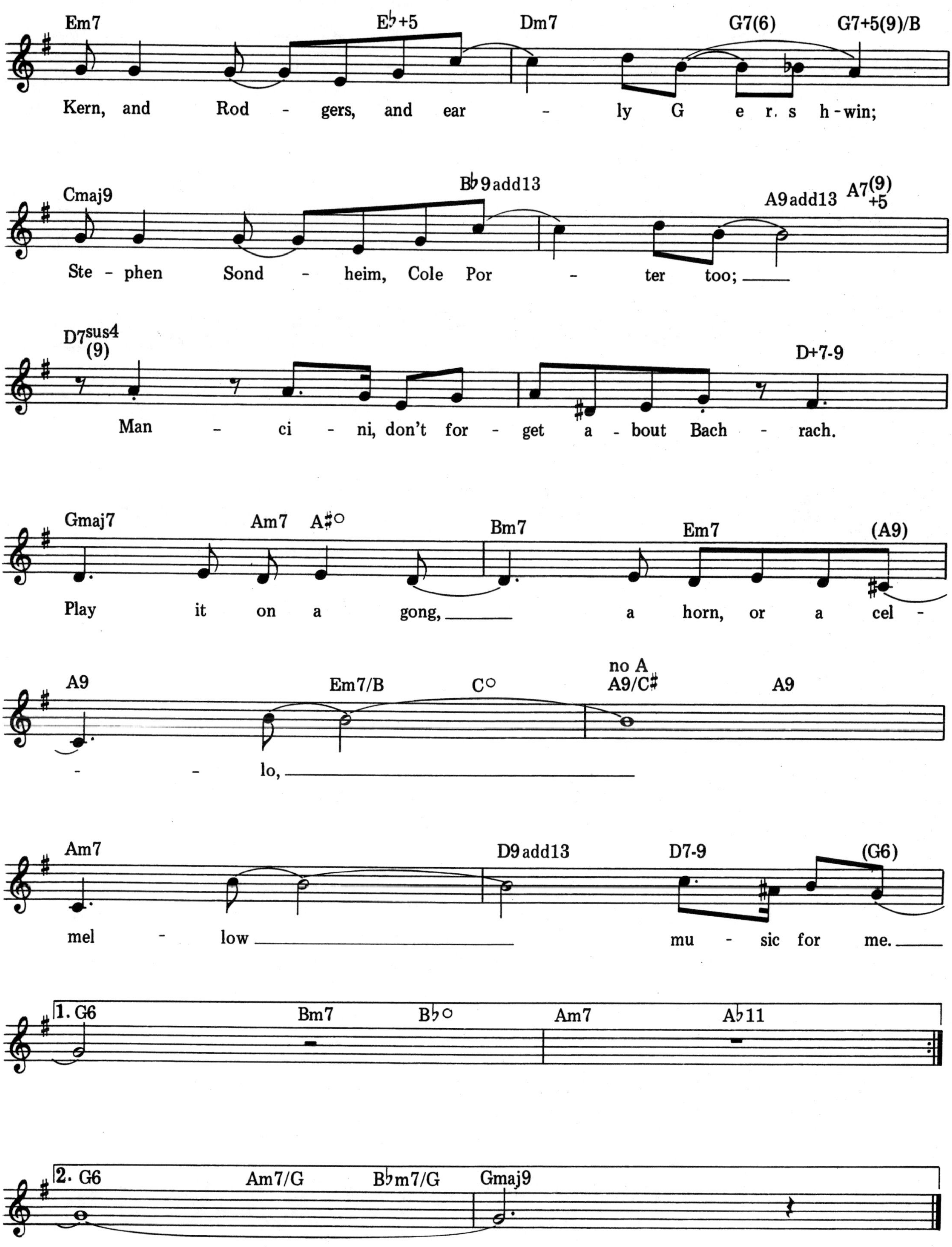
Em7 E♭+5 Dm7 G7(6) G7+5(9)/B
Kern, and Rod - gers, and ear - ly G e r. s h - win;
Cmaj9 B♭9add13 A9add13 A7(9) +5
Ste - phen Sond - heim, Cole Por - ter too;
D7sus4 (9) D+7-9
Man - ci - ni, don't for - get a - bout Bach - rach.
Gmaj7 Am7 A♯○ Bm7 Em7 (A9)
Play it on a gong, a horn, or a cel -
A9 Em7/B C○ no A A9/C♯ A9
- - lo,
Am7 D9add13 D7-9 (G6)
mel - low mu - sic for me.
1. G6 Bm7 B♭○ Am7 A♭11
2. G6 Am7/G B♭m7/G Gmaj9

# "Mel's Pick"

Dedicated to the famous Guitarist Mel Bay

Sheet Music

Composed by Matt Dennis
A.S.C.A.P.

Instrumental
Medium tempo - steady beat

C6
C♯°
G6/D
B7-9
Em
B+/D♯
Em7/D♮
no A
A9/C♯
Am7
D7sus4
D7-9
G
C9
G
G♯°
Am7
D7sus4(9)
D7-9
add13
G6
1.
E+7-9
A9
D+7-9
2.
C9add13
Gmaj9

# "Mel's Pick"

Comping Arr.

Composed by
Matt Dennis
A.S.C.A.P.

Used by permission

no G
G6(9)
Gadd9
G♯°
Am9
D7sus9
add13
D7-9
G6
Am7
B♭°
G7/B
C6
C♯°
G6add9/D
nc
B7-9
D♯Bass
Em
B7-9/D♯
no E
Em7/D♮
no A
A9/C♯
Am7

nc
3
D7sus4
no D
D+7-9/C
G6
C9
Gmaj9
G6
G♯○
Am7
Am11
G
1.
no D
D7-9
D Bass
add13 A♭Bass
G6
E+7-9
A9
D+7-9
2.
no C
C9add13/B♭
no G
Gmaj9add6/B
Gmaj9

# "Mel's Pick"

**Improv. Arr.**

a "two chorus" arr.

Composed by Matt Dennis
A.S.C.A.P.

Used by permission

(G♯○)
Am9
nc
A♭ Bass
A♭9
nc
G Bass
G
A∅
B♭○
G7/B
G Bass
G7sus4
add 9, 13
G7-9
C6add9
C6
C♯○
nc
D Bass
G6
G
B♭
Am7
Gm
C9add13
B9add13
Em
B+/D♯
Em7/D
A9/C♯
nc
Am7 Bm C6
C♯○
D7sus4
(9)
D7-9, ♯11
add13
Gmaj9
no C
C9add13
B♭
nc
G Bass

Gmaj9
Bm7
B♭m7
Am9
Bm7
C6
no A
A9/C♯
nc
D Bass
D7sus4 add9
B+7/A
no E
(B7/A)E7-9/G♯
no A
A9/G
no D
D7-9/F♯
nc
2nd Chorus
Gmaj9 add13
nc
C9add13
nc
G
F/A
no G
Gmaj7/B
E♭7sus4 add9
Am7
D7
(9)
Cm6/A
D7-9
G
E7
A7
D7
G Bass
G7(6)

C9
Gmaj7(6)
G Bass
Bm7
B♭m7
Am7
L.H.
nc
B Bass
C Bass
C♯Bass
D Bass
D7sus4
(9)D7-9, ♯11
add13
G7add13
A♭9/G
add13/G♭
G9add13/F♮
G+7-9
G Bass
no C
C6/E
Cm7
F7add13
F♯○
nc
Gmaj9
G Bass
Dm7
G9♯11
B+7♯9
(Em)
E Bass
B+/D♯
no E
Em7
D Bass
no A
A9/C♯
nc
A Bass
B Bass
C Bass
C♯Bass
(D7sus4)
D Bass
nc
no G
Gmaj9/F♯

Please note that where the sheet music, comping and lead sheet arrangements have 1st and 2nd endings at the end of the chorus, the improv arrangement, being inventive, carries on from the 1st chorus directly into a 2nd chorus, showing that when you are inspired in your improvisation you can continue with another chorus. No two choruses need sound alike, that's the true spark of being original with your improv, and that's when it's fun to play. The 4 bar "intro" is to set the mood and tempo of the piece, so when you start the chorus there's a comfortable groove for the improv.

# "Mel's Pick"

**Lead Sheet**

Composed by Matt Dennis
A.S.C.A.P.

C6
C♯°
G6/D
G
B7-9
Em
B+/D♯
Em7/D
no A
A9/C♯
Am7
D7sus4
D7-9
G
C9
G
G♯°
Am7
D7sus4(9)
add13
D7-9
G6
1.
E+7 -9
A9
D+7-9
2.
C9
Gmaj9

# "What Can I Say?"

Sheet Music

Words by Tom Adair
A.S.C.A.P.

Music by Matt Dennis
A.S.C.A.P.

Dm7 G7 Dm7 G7
why did I let you tear me a - part?
Cmaj7 Dm7 Em7 E♭°
I could have let you step on my heart, and I'd
Dm7 G7 Dm7 G7 Cmaj7 C6
wind up a - lone with no - bo - dy to turn to,
B♭m7 E♭7 B♭m7 E♭7 B♭m7 E♭7
oh my! Your kind of love is fleet - ing as spring,

A♭maj7 B♭m7 Cm7 B° B♭m7 E♭7
once it has gone for get the whole thing! Your kind of love
B♭m7 E♭7 E♭m6/C Bass F7
makes my heart want to cry.
B♭m7 C° D♭m6 E♭°
La - dy luck can turn her face from me,
A° B♭m7 D♭m7 D♭m6
life can steal my fin - al ace from me.

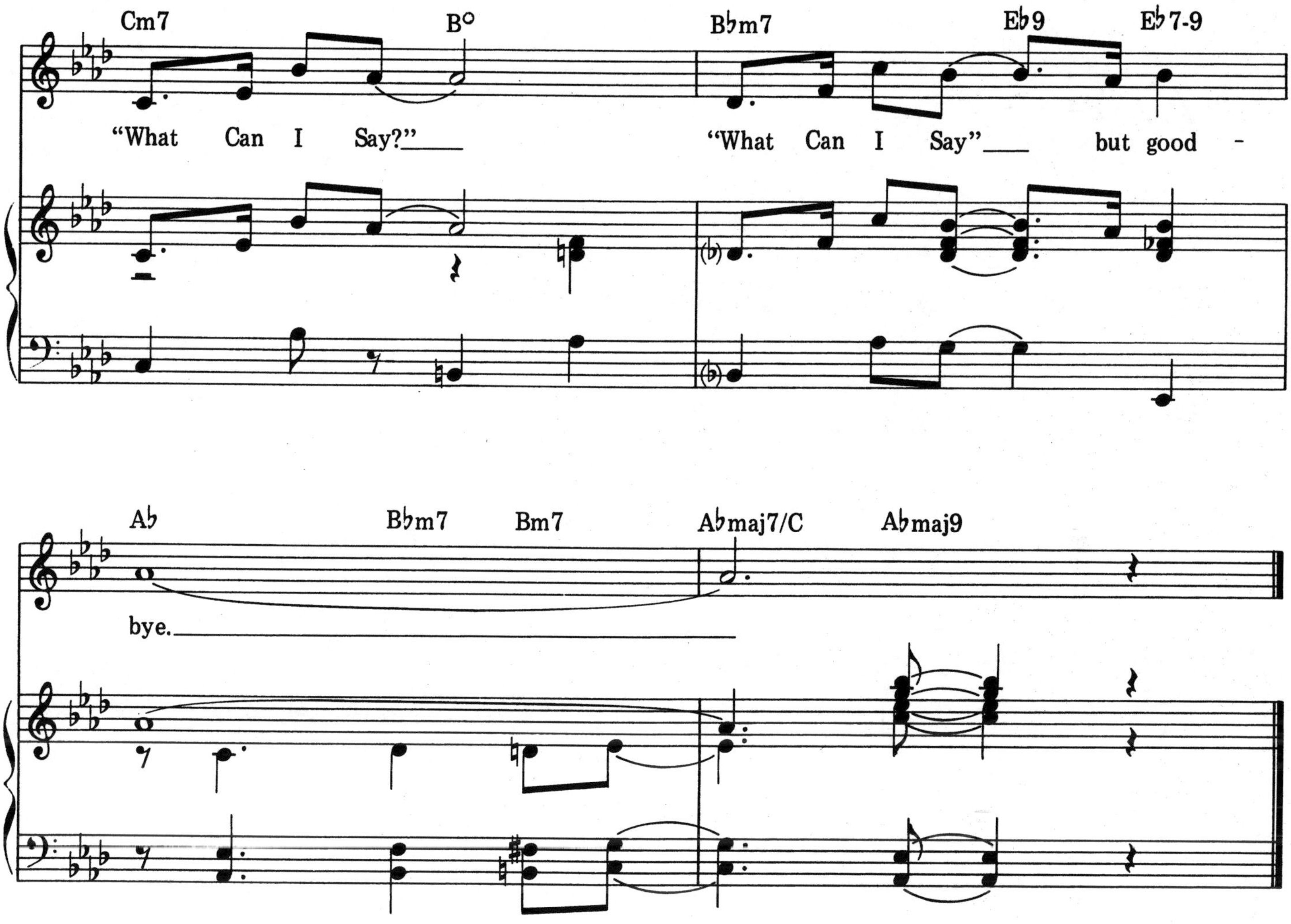


The lyric (words) will give you the rhythm feeling, along with the actual notation of the melody, and help you to understand the phrasing. This will enable you to interpret this song with proper rhythmic and emotional expression . . . helping you with the phrasing.

A lyric, when available, can be a help in understanding the complete message of the song . . . even when just sight reading the piece. By the time you get to the "comping" and "improv" versions the basic thought or idea of the song and it's form should be quite clear. Really make an effort to memorize the sheet music.

No 1st and 2nd endings in this arrangement . . . the melody, with lyric, finishes naturally.

# "What Can I Say?"

Comping

Words by Tom Adair
A.S.C.A.P.

Music by Matt Dennis
A.S.C.A.P.

G7
Cmaj7
Dm7
Em7
E♭°
Dm7
G7
Dm7
G7
Cmaj7
C6
B♭m7
E♭7
B♭m7
E♭7
B♭m7
E♭7
A♭maj7
B♭m7
Cm7
B°
B♭m7
E♭7
B♭m7

E♭7
E♭m6/C
F7
B♭ Bass
B♭m7
C°
D♭6
E♭°
C°
A Bass
A°
B♭m7
D♭m9
D♭m6
C Bass
Cm7
B°
B♭Bass
B♭m7
E♭7-9
A♭6
A♭maj7
B♭m7
Bm7
Cm7
A♭maj9

# "What Can I Say?"

Jazz Improv

Words: Tom Adair
A.S.C.A.P.

Music: Matt Dennis
A.S.C.A.P.

Dm7
no G
G+7-9/F
G Bass
no G
G+7-9
F
no C
Cmaj9/E
nc
Em7
E♭m7
Dm9
no G
G7add13/B
Dm7
G7add13
no G
G+7-9/F
no C
C6add9/E
nc
B♭m9
no E♭
E♭7-9
E♭ Bass
B♭m9
E♭9
B♭m9
A9
A♭maj9
B♭m7add11
Bm7Cm7
Bm7
B♭m7
E♭9

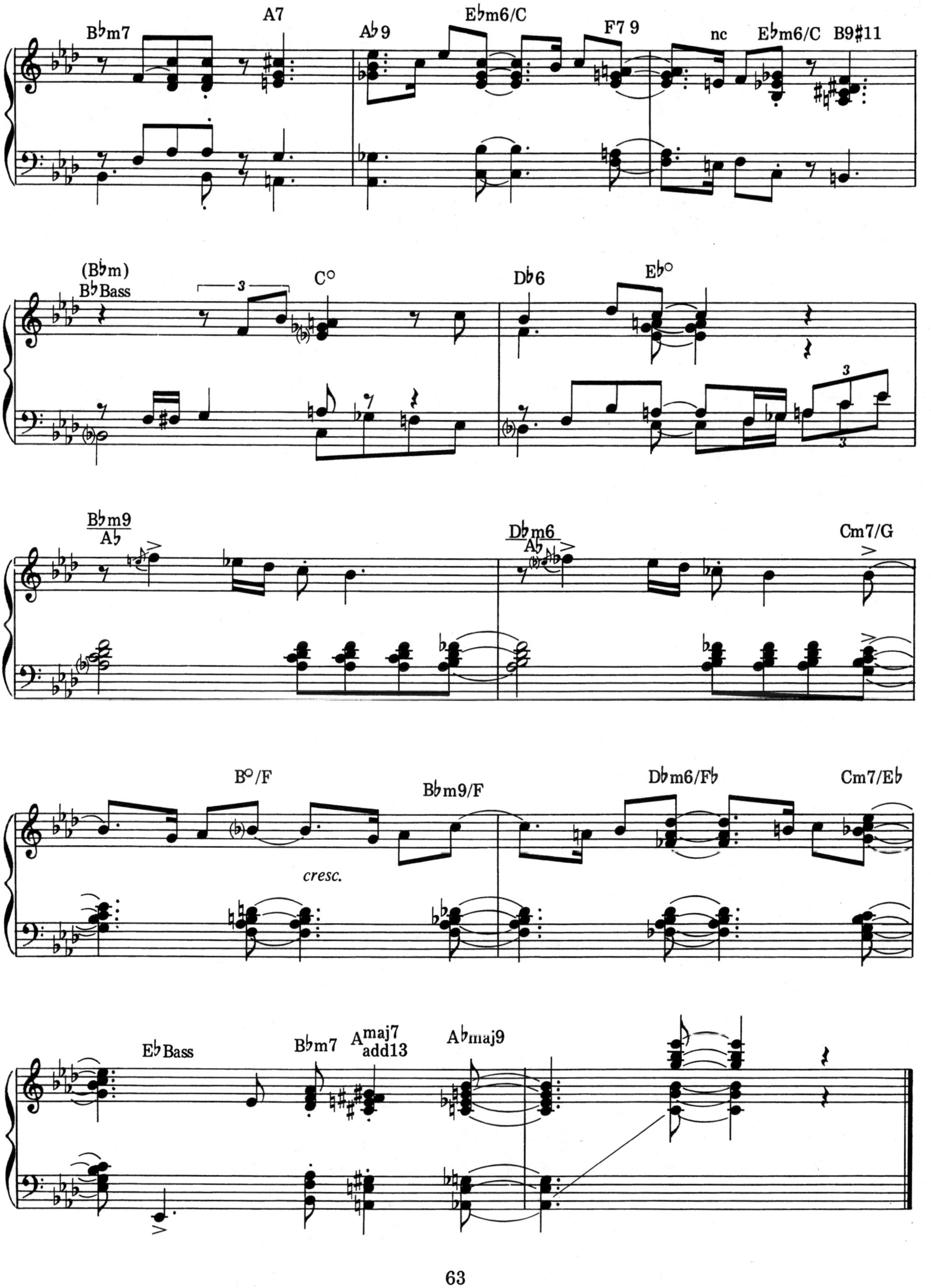
B♭m7
A7
A♭9
E♭m6/C
F7 9
nc
E♭m6/C
B9♯11
(B♭m)
B♭Bass
3
C°
D♭6
E♭°
3
3
B♭m9/A♭
D♭m6/A♭
Cm7/G
B°/F
B♭m9/F
cresc.
D♭m6/F♭
Cm7/E♭
E♭Bass
B♭m7
Amaj7 add13
A♭maj9

Lead Sheet

# "What Can I Say?"

Words: Tom Adair
A.S.C.A.P.

Music: Matt Dennis
A.S.C.A.P.

Dm7 G7 Cmaj7 C6 B♭m7 E♭7
with no - bo - dy to turn to, oh my!
B♭m7 E♭7 B♭m7 E♭7
Your kind of love is fleet - ing as Spring,
A♭maj7 B♭m7 Cm7 B°
once it has gone for - get the whole thing!
B♭m7 E♭7 B♭m7 E♭7
Your kind of love makes my heart want to
E♭m6
C Bass
F7 B♭m7 C°
cry. La - dy luck can
D♭6 E♭° A° B♭m7
turn her face me, life can steal my
D♭m7 D♭m6 Cm7 B°
fin - al ace me. "What Can I Say?"
B♭m7 E♭9 E♭7♭9 A♭ B♭m7 Bm7 A♭maj7
C
A♭maj9
"What Can I Say" but good - bye.

Sheet Music

# "Angel Eyes"

Lyric by: Earl K. Brent
A.S.C.A.P.

Music by: Matt Dennis
A.S.C.A.P.

Dm Dm7/C B♭9 A+7-9 Dm Dm7/C Bm7-5 Em7 A7-5 A7-9
old dev-il sent, they glow un-bear-a-bly bright.
Dm Dm7 B° B♭ø Dm Dm7/C B♭9 Dm B♭9 A+7-9
Need I say that my love's mis-spent, mis-spent with An-gel Eyes to-night.
D Ped. (opt.)
Dm Cm9 F7-9 B♭maj9 Dm9 G+7-9
So drink up all you peo-ple,
Cm9 F7-9 B♭maj9 B♭6 Bm9 E7-9
or-der an-y-thing you see. Have fun you hap-py

or Ebm11
or Ab+7-9
Amaj7 A6 D#m11 G#+7-9 Em11 A+7-9
peo-ple, the drink and the laugh's on me.
Dm Dm7 B° Bbø Dm Dm7 Bb9 A+7-9 Dm Dm7 Bm7-5
Par-don me, but I got-ta run, the fact's un-com-mon-ly clear.
D Ped. (opt.)
Em7 A7-5 A7 Dm Dm7 B° Bbø Dm Dm7/C Bb9
Got-ta find who's now "num-ber one" and
D Ped.(opt.)
Dm Bb9 A+7-9 Dm Bb9 A+7+9 Dm add13 add maj7/9/11
why my An-gel Eyes ain't here. 'Scuse me while I dis-a - ppear.
rit.
rit.
R.H.
L.H.
L.H.

# "Angel Eyes"

Comping Arr.

Lyric: Earl K. Brent
Music: Matt Dennis
A.S.C.A.P.

Slowly-with a beat
(cued-in melody)

3
Dm/A
C Bass
B♭9
add13
A+7-9
Dm9
no D
Dm6
add9, 11/B
Dm6/B
E7-9
(13)
E+7
A7sus4
(9)
nc
A7-9 D Bass
Dm7
D°add9
E♭/D
Dm
nc
B♭Bass
B♭9
add13
Dm
E7
A7
Dm7
nc
Cm9
F7-9
add13
Dm7
G7-9
add13
nc
3
Cm7
F7-9
add13
nc
B♭maj7
Cm7
Dm7
Bm11
E7-9
add13

or Ebm11
or Ab+7-9
Amaj9
A6
nc
D#Bass D#m11 G#+7-9
nc
E Bass
Em11
A+7-9
nc
3
D Bass
Dm7
D°
A7-9
Dm6
Bb7add13 A+7
Dm11
C Bass
nc
B Bass
Dm6/B
E Bass
Gm6/E
A+7-9
nc
D Bass
Fmaj7/D
Emaj7/D
Ebmaj7/D
Dm7
C6
Bb7sus4 add9
Bb9
rit.
E Bass E+7-9
A+7-9
Dm6nc
rit.
Bb9add13/Ab
Bb Bass
A+7 +9,11 /G
A Bass
nc
Dm6 add maj7/9
slowly
Pedal

# "Angel Eyes"

**Jazz Improv**

**Matt Dennis Arr.**

**Lyrics: Earl K. Brent**
**Music: Matt Dennis**
**A.S.C.A.P.**

Dm
Dm7
B♭9 (13)
A7+9 (13)
(A+7-9)
Dm(9)
B♭7sus4 (9)
A-7-9
nc D Bass
nc
Dm6
E°
Dm6/F
no A A7-9/G
B♭9
A7-9 add11
Dm
(addmaj7)
(Dm7)
(Dm6)
B♭9,+11
E7-9 add13
A7-9 add11
Dm6
Cm7
E♭°
Dm7
no G G+7-9/F
mf

add13
F7
Cm9
E♭m9
Dm7
B♭maj7
Cm7
Dm7
nc
Bm7
E7-9
nc
Amaj7
A6
nc
no E♭
E♭m9/G♭
no A♭
A♭+7,-9,+11 /G♭
A♭7-9
nc
no E
Em9/G
no A
A+7,-9,+11/G
A7-9
dim.
Dm
B♭m9
A7+11
p
D Bass
Dm6 Cmaj7Dm7 Cmaj7 Dm6
B♭13,+11
A7-9 add13
D Pedal
D Bass
Dm7
B♭ 9,+11, 13
A7sus4 add9
A7-9+11

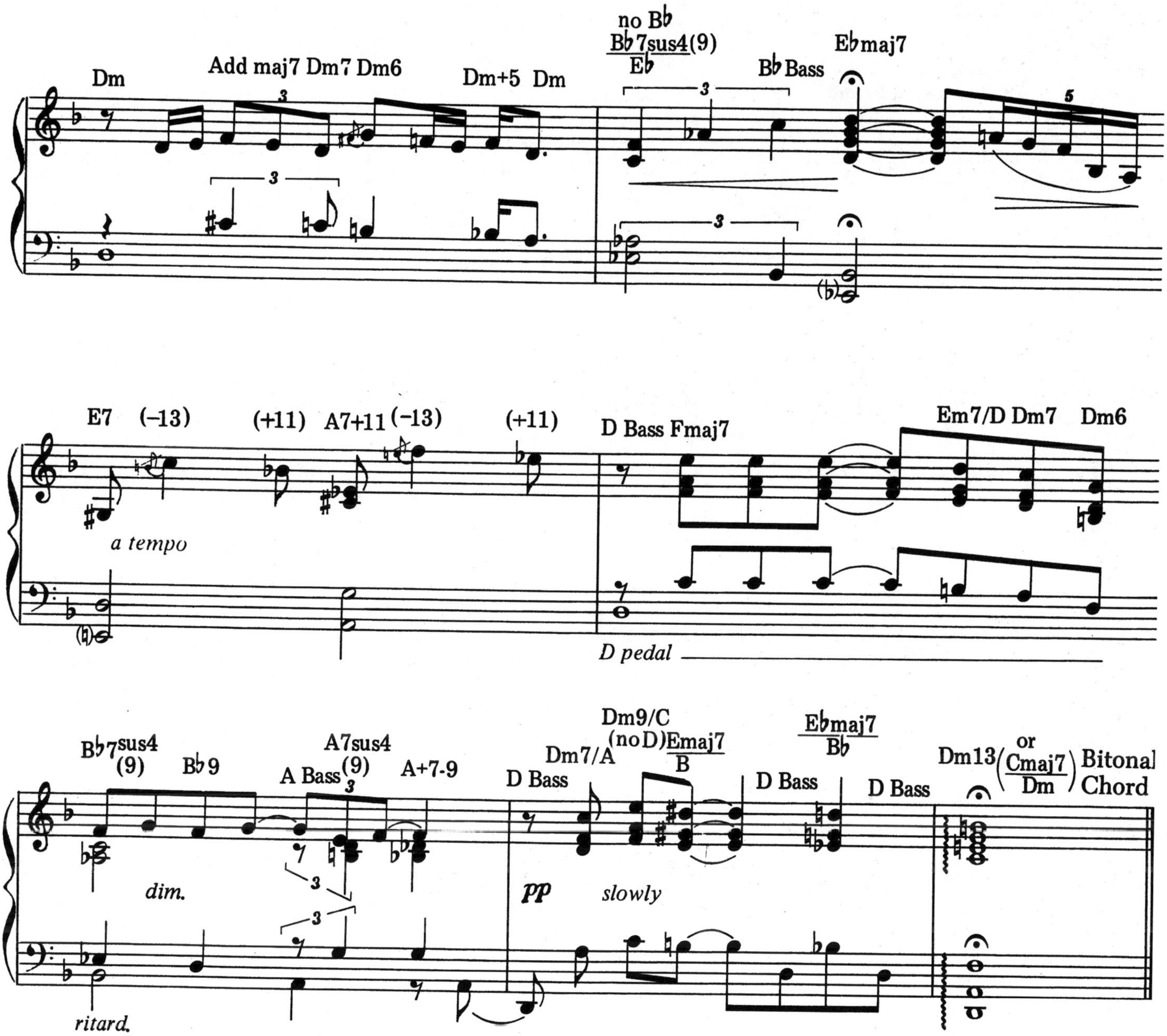


* The countless times I have improvised on this song of mine I always seem to approach the song with a new concept, changing the melody and altering or substituting chords . . . sometimes even enharmonically . . . But always relative to the original, no matter how far away I may seem to stray from the original. It can be an inspiring experience, with all the exploratory improvisation.

Lead Sheet
(For Improvisation)

# "Angel Eyes"

Lyric by Earl K. Brent
A.S.C.A.P.

Music by Matt Dennis
A.S.C.A.P.

Dm Bb9 A+7-9 Dm
spent with An - gel Eyes to - night. So
Cm9 F7-9 Bbmaj9 Dm9 G+7-9
drink up all you peo - ple
Cm9 F7-9 Bbmaj9 Bb6 Bm9 E7-9
or - der an - y - thing you see. Have fun you hap - py
or Ebm11
or Ab+7-9
Amaj7 A6 D#m11 G#+7-9 Em11 A+7-9
peo - ple, the drink and the laugh's on me.
Dm Dm7 B° Bbø Dm Dm7/C Bb9 A+7-9
Par - don me, but I got - ta run,
D Pedal (opt.)
Dm Dm7/C Bm7add11 Em7 A7-5 A7 Dm Dm7 B° Bbø
the fact's un - com - mon - ly clear, Got - ta find who's
D Pedal (opt.)
Dm Dm7/C Bb9 Dm Bb9 A+7-9
now "num - ber one" and why my An - gel Eyes ain't here
Dm Bb9 A+7+9 Dm6 9 add maj7/9/11
'scuse me while I dis - a - ppear.

# "Laughin' At Life"

**Sheet Music**

**Instrumental**

Composed by Matt Dennis
A.S.C.A.P.

Easy jazz tempo

E+7+9
Am7
D+7-9
Dm6/B
E+7add+11
Am7
nc
A♭7+9
G6
nc
Dm9
G7-9 nc
Cmaj9
C6 nc
Dm7
G7-9 nc
Cmaj7Dm7Em7
nc
Fm9
B♭7-9 nc
E♭maj9
E♭6 nc
Am7 Bm7
Cm7
nc
D7-9,+11
add13
(melody )

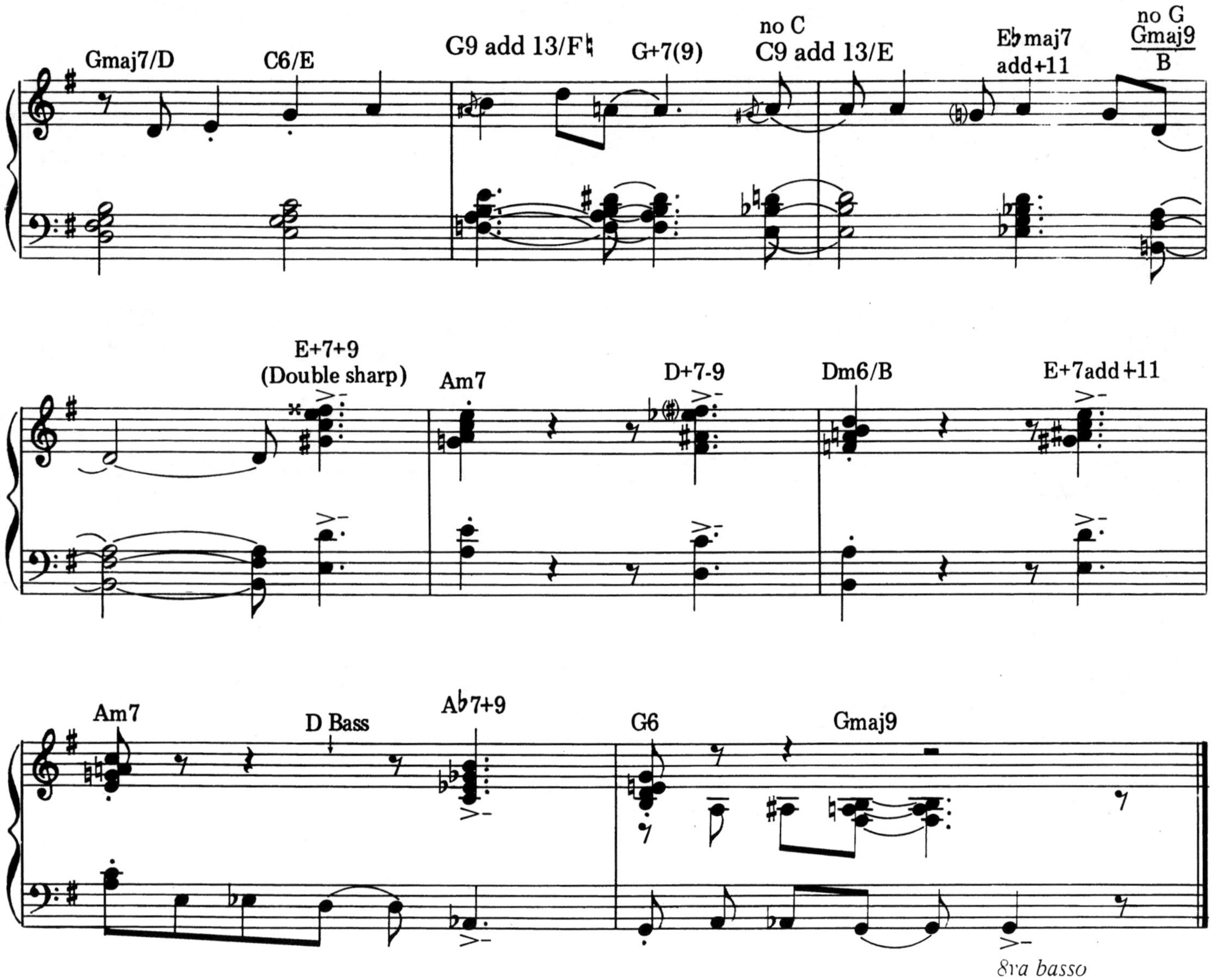


Some choice chords used here, in this instrumental sheet music arrangement. Note the E+7+9 chord in the 4th measure, and where repeated in measures 12 and 28 . . . the melody note in treble clef is an "f double sharp." I call this the "Gershwin chord," since George Gershwin used this harmony in his music. Other interesting chords shown in this arrangement and piece are the C9 add 13, with an E Bass, no C in this particular voicing; the A7 sus 4, add 9 & 13; A♭ 7+9 (Gershwin, again); and D7 - 9, + 11, add 13. Usually such chords are saved for an "Improv" arrangement, however the sheet music shows them from the start, in this case. When improvising on a piece you will, at times, use "substitution" or "altered" chords, improving on the original sheet arrangement. Such chords are formed in a flattering way to the original, by adding notes in extended harmony, or making changes depending upon how you "voice" both hands as you improvise . . . inventing your own melodic line.

# "Laughin' At Life"

Comping Arr.

Composed by Matt Dennis
A.S.C.A.P.

Used by permission

Dm7
no G
G+7/F♮
no C
C9/E
E♭maj7
no G
Gmaj9/D
nc
E+7-9
Am7 nc
D+7-9
Dm6
B nc
E+7-9
Am7 nc
A♭7+9
G6
no D
Dm9/F♮
no G
G7-9/F♮
G Bass
no C
Cmaj9/E
C6/E
G Bass
Dm7
no G
G7-9/D
Cmaj7 Dm7 Em7
nc

no F
Fm9/A♭
no B♭
B♭7-9/A♭
nc
no E♭
E♭maj9/G
E♭6/G
nc
Am7 Bm7 Cm7
nc
(Am) nc
D7-9,+11
add13
Gmaj9
Am7
Dm9
no G
G9+5/F♮
G Bass
no C
C9add13
E
E♭maj7
no G
Gmaj9/B
E+7-9
Am7 nc
D+7-9
Dm6/B
nc
E+7+9
Am7 nc
A♭7+9
G6 nc
Gmaj9
add13

# "Laughin' At Life"

**Jazz Improv**

Composed by Matt Dennis
A.S.C.A.P.

Used by permission

E+7-9
Am7
D7sus4 add9
D+7-9
Dm6/B
F9+11
E+7-9
nc A Bass
Am7
A♭7
G6
nc
Dm7
no G G7-9add13
Em7
nc
add13 A7-9
nc D Bass
Dm9
G7-9 add13
nc C Bass
Cmaj9
nc
F Bass
Fm
B♭7-9
nc
G Bass
Gm
Cm7
nc
Am9
Bm7
Cm7
nc
no A add maj7 Am
Am7
D+7-9

<u>"Extended ending"</u>

Instead of the usual ending of this piece at the 32nd measure according to the sheet music, a "surprise" ending can be started at the 32nd measure, interupting the natural ending, providing a spontaneous, improvised feeling for the final 4 measures. This is a good effect, and often used with jazz standards.

# "Laughin' At Life"

Lead Sheet

Composed by Matt Dennis
A.S.C.A.P.

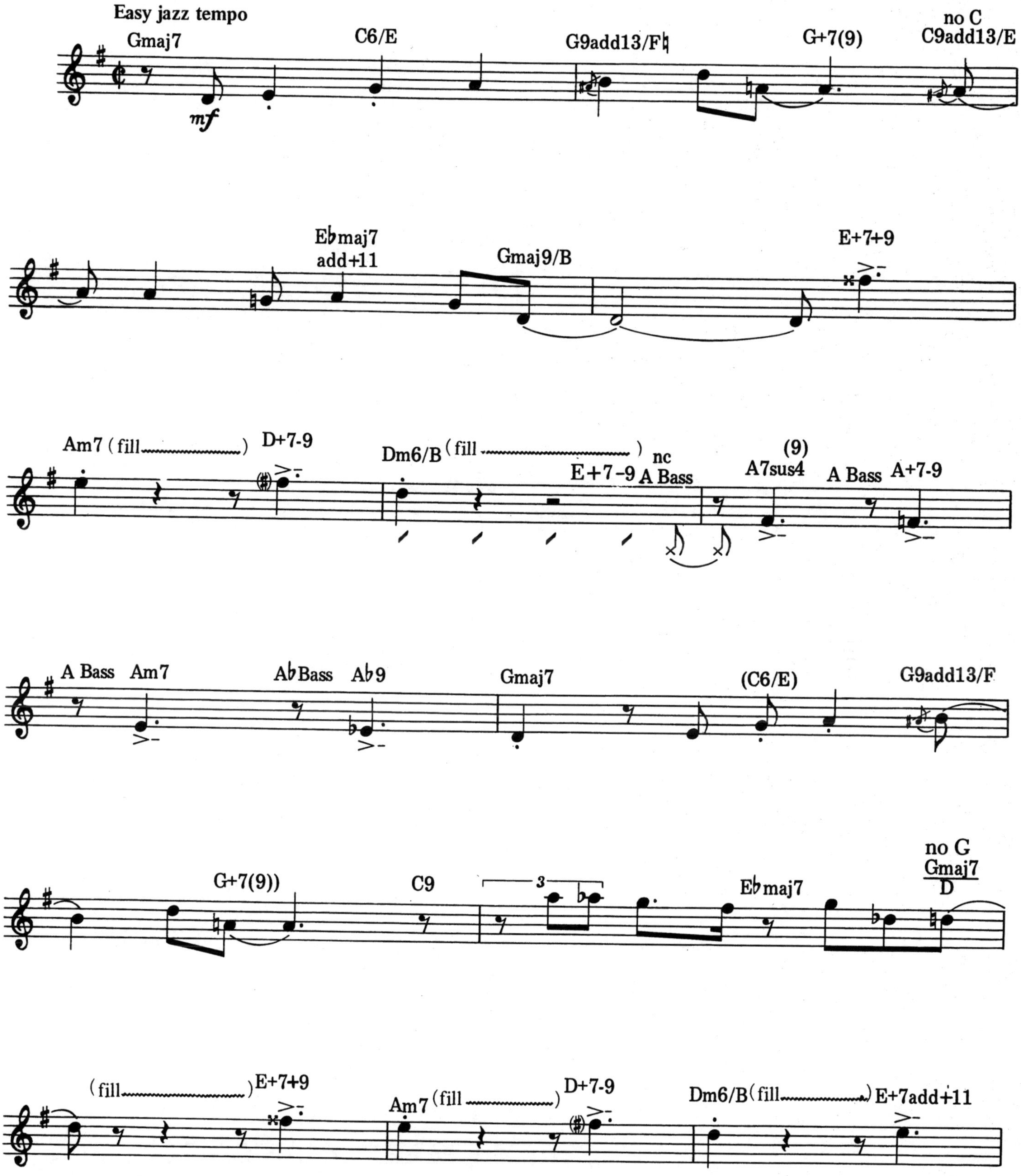

Am7 (fill )
A♭7+9
G6 (fill )
nc
Dm9
G7-9
no C
Cmaj9
C6
Dm7
G7-9
nc
Cmaj7 Dm7 Em7
nc
Fm9
B♭7-9
(Beats)
E♭maj9
E♭6
nc
(fill )
Am7 Bm7 Cm7
nc
(fill D13-9 )
(Am7)
Gmaj7
C6/E
G9add13/F♮
C+7(0)
no C
C9add13/E
E♭maj7
add+11
no G
Gmaj9/B
E+7+9
Am7
D+7-9
Dm6/B
E+7add+11
Am7 (fill )
D Bass
A♭7+9
G6 (fill )
Gmaj9